KU-196-739

www.BillieBBrown.com

The Beautiful Haircut
published in 2010 by
Hardie Grant Egmont
Ground Floor, Building 1, 658 Church Street
Richmond, Victoria 3121, Australia
www.hardiegrantegmont.com.au

All rights reserved. No part of this publication may be reproduced,
stored in a retrieval system or transmitted in any form by any means without
the prior permission of the publishers and copyright owner.

A CiP record for this title is available from the National Library of Australia

Text copyright © 2010 Sally Rippin
Illustration copyright © 2010 Aki Fukuoka
Logo and design copyright © 2010 Hardie Grant Egmont

Design and typeset by Stephanie Spartels

7 9 10 8 6

Printed in Australia by Griffin Press, an accredited ISO AS/NZS
14001:2004 Environmental Management System printer.

FSC
www.fsc.org
MIX
Paper from
responsible sources
FSC® C009448

The paper this book is printed on is certified against the
Forest Stewardship Council® Standards. Griffin Press holds
FSC chain of custody certification SGS-COC-005088. FSC
promotes environmentally responsible, socially beneficial
and economically viable management of the world's forests

The Beautiful Haircut

By Sally Rippin

Illustrated by Aki Fukuoka

hardie grant EGMONT

Chapter One

Billie B Brown has three long-haired dolls, twelve sparkly hairclips and one pink comb. Do you know what the B in Billie B Brown stands for?

Beautiful.

Billie B Brown is
playing hairdressers today.
Hairdressers make people
look beautiful.

Jack is Billie's best friend.
He lives next door.
Billie and Jack play
together every day.

Box of sparkly
hairclips

Three long-haired dolls

Pink comb

3

If Jack wants to build a cubby house, Billie helps him. If Billie wants to play soccer, Jack plays too.

But Jack doesn't want to play with Billie today.

'Why don't you want me to do your hair?' Billie asks. 'I can make you look beautiful.'

'No, thanks,' Jack frowns.

'Why not?' asks Billie.

'I am a great hairdresser.
I can make anyone look
beautiful. Long hair,
short hair, boy, girl.'

Jack scrunches up his face. 'I don't want to look beautiful, Billie. I want to look cool. Can't we play something else?'

'No, I want to play hairdressers,' Billie says **crossly**. 'If you don't want to play with me you can go home.'

Jack stares at Billie.

Billie stares at Jack. Then

Jack stands up and walks

out of Billie's bedroom.

Billie looks out her
bedroom window.
She sees Jack walk
outside into the garden.

There is a hole in the
fence between Jack's
house and Billie's house.
Jack squeezes through
the hole and runs home.

Billie feels very **annoyed**.

She and Jack always play together! It was Billie's turn to choose the game so she chose hairdressers. Jack didn't even try to let Billie do his hair!

Billie knows Jack will be back soon. They never stay **mad** at each other for long.

Anyway, Billie doesn't have time to **worry** about Jack now. She is a hairdresser, and she has lots of customers!

Chapter Two

Billie looks at her dolls.
They all have long hair.

'I don't need Jack to play
hairdressers,' she says
to them. 'I have you.
OK, who is next?'

Billie picks up a doll.
'Claudia! Look at your
hair. It's such a mess!
I will fix it for you.'

When Billie's doll
Claudia was new, she
had lovely long hair.
Now it is like a yellow
bush. Long hair is very
difficult to look after.

You have to brush it
a lot. This can be a little
bit boring.

Billie puts some clips in Claudia's hair. 'Mmm, that's better,' Billie says. Claudia looks beautiful.

Next it is Tomoko's turn. Tomoko has dark hair just like Billie's. Tomoko's hair used to be shiny and smooth, but one day Billie accidentally dropped some glue in it.

Now one side is smooth
and one side is knotted.

Not to worry. Billie is
such a good hairdresser
that she can make any
hair look great. She puts
a sparkly clip into
Tomoko's hair.
Yes, that's
much better!

Billie's last doll used to be called Barbara but now everyone calls her Stinky. Stinky used to have long ginger curls but now they are just a teensy bit green.

Billie left Stinky down in the bottom of the garden for three whole weeks.

Stinky is still beautiful
but now she is a little bit
mouldy and, well, a little
bit **stinky**.

Stinky looks very pretty
with sparkly hairclips in
her hair, doesn't she?

The dolls are very good customers. They sit very still and they don't talk.

Much better than Jack, Billie thinks.

But soon Billie starts to get bored. Billie is a very good hairdresser, but real hairdressers don't just put clips in hair.

They don't just brush and comb and smooth.

Real hairdressers **cut**.

Billie looks for her purple plastic scissors in her pencil case. Billie's scissors are very good at cutting paper. She hopes they will be good at cutting hair, too.

Billie puts Claudia on
her special hairdressing
seat. She tries to cut
a little bit off the bottom
of Claudia's hair.
But nothing happens.

She tries Tomoko next, and then Stinky. But it's no good.

Billie's plastic scissors are good for cutting paper, but terrible for cutting hair.

Billie frowns. How can she be a hairdresser if she can't even cut hair?

Then, Billie has an idea.

Chapter Three

Billie goes into the bathroom. She opens up the drawer and sees a shiny pair of scissors.

Billie is not allowed to touch the kitchen scissors.

But these scissors are different, Billie decides. They are only little scissors. Perfect for giving little haircuts.

Billie thinks she is probably allowed to use these.

Billie picks up the little scissors.

She hopes they will be better than her purple plastic ones. They look very sharp. She decides to test them out.

Billie holds up one of her pigtails and gives a little snip.

Oh yes, they are very sharp. Billie's pigtail falls into the sink! It lies there looking like a little furry mouse.

Oh dear. Billie looks in the mirror. Now she only has one pigtail.

27

Billie doesn't look beautiful at all. In fact, she looks silly! She can't walk around with just one pigtail. Everyone will laugh at her!

So Billie snips off the other pigtail. Now both sides look the same.

Two little pigtails lie in the sink.

Billie is amazed at how easily they came off. She wishes she could stick them back on again. Billie liked her two pigtails. Now she has none!

Billie looks in the mirror. Tears roll down her cheeks. She wishes she had never found those horrible sharp scissors!

She wishes she had her
two little pigtails back!
She stares at her funny
haircut and tries to
stop crying.

Just then, Billie sees
someone else in the
mirror. It's Jack!

'Billie! What have you
done?' says Jack.

His eyes are as big as tennis balls. 'You cut off your pigtails!'

Billie covers her hair with her hands. 'Don't tell Mum!' she pleads. 'I'm going to be in so much trouble!'

'But what are you going to do?' asks Jack. 'You can't hide your hair forever!'

'I'll wear a hat!' says Billie.

'Until it grows back.'

'Don't be silly,' Jack says.
'You have to tell your
mum. She'll know what
to do.'

Billie hangs her head.
She knows that Jack
is right. She feels very
nervous. But with Jack
beside her, it's not so bad.

They walk into the
kitchen to find Billie's
mum.

Chapter Four

Billie's mum is sitting at
the table reading the paper.
She looks up as Billie and
Jack come into the room.
'Oh, Billie!' she gasps.
'What have you done?'

Billie scrunches up
her face. She covers her
eyes with her hands.
Then she starts to cry.

'I was playing hairdressers,' she sobs.

Billie's mum stands up and pulls Billie into a hug. 'My silly Billie,' she sighs. She ruffles Billie's funny hair.

'You're not cross?' Billie asks. She looks up at her mum with wet eyes.

'Well, yes, a little bit,'
Billie's mum frowns.
'You know you're not
allowed to play with
scissors!'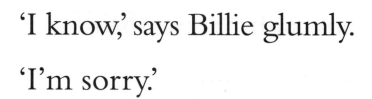

'I know,' says Billie glumly.
'I'm sorry.'

But then Billie's mum
gives a small smile. 'Do you
know what?' she says.

'When I was a little girl I did exactly the same thing.' She gives Billie a squeeze.

'Really?' Billie asks, amazed. 'You cut off your pigtails?'

'Yep. Except I looked much worse than you,' Billie's mum laughs.

'My hair was sticking up everywhere! You've still got plenty of hair left. But it looks like we'll have to take you to a real hairdresser, hey?'

'I miss my pigtails,' Billie sighs.

'Don't worry,' Billie's mum says.

41

'Glenda will give you a great haircut. She can make anyone look beautiful!'

'Can she do cool haircuts, too?' Jack asks.

'You bet,' says Billie's mum.

'Great!' says Jack.
'Then I'll ask mum if I can get one, too.'

'Let's go, then,' says
Billie's mum.

Billie hugs her mum.
Jack was right, she thinks.
Mum did know what to do.

44